Carmelita's Cabbage

Written by Cushla Brown
Illustrated by Rod Proud

Carmelita liked to eat cabbage.
So she got a little cabbage seed.

She put the cabbage seed in a little pot.

"Grow, little cabbage seed," said Carmelita.
"Grow into a big green cabbage
that I can eat for my dinner."

On Monday, Carmelita put water on her little cabbage seed. "Grow," she said.

On Tuesday, Carmelita looked at her little cabbage seed. It had a little shoot.

On Wednesday, Carmelita's cabbage had a leaf.

On Thursday, Carmelita's cabbage had two leaves.
"Grow, little cabbage," said Carmelita.

On Friday,
Carmelita's cabbage had ten leaves.
"Grow into a big cabbage," said Carmelita.

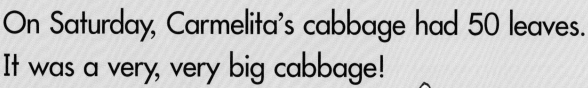

On Saturday, Carmelita's cabbage had 50 leaves.
It was a very, very big cabbage!

Carmelita said,
"In one more day, I am going to pick you
and eat you up for my dinner."

On Sunday,
Carmelita went to pick her cabbage.
It had grown bigger and bigger.
It had 100 leaves.

"I will have a very big dinner now," said Carmelita.

9

"You can't pick this cabbage,"
said a white butterfly. "I live on this cabbage.
I live here with these little white butterflies."

"I live here, too," said a caterpillar.
"So do these little caterpillars."

"I live here, too," said a little red ladybug.
"You cannot pick this cabbage.
These little ladybugs
live on this cabbage with me."

"Oh, no!" said Carmelita.
"How can I pick this cabbage now?
I will have to plant a new cabbage seed."

So she did.

Word Count	240
Genre	Recount (Fantasy)
High-Frequency Words	had, how, now, one, put, very

The McGraw·Hill Companies

ISBN 1-4045-5255-3

90000>

9 781404 552555

Mc Graw Hill **Wright Group**